For Marianne and Ciaran
M.W.

To Helen Walpole
B.F.

First published 1990
by Walker Books Ltd, 87 Vauxhall Walk
London SE11 5HJ

This edition published 1999

2 4 6 8 10 9 7 5 3 1

This book has been typeset in Goudy.

Printed in Hong Kong

British Library Cataloguing in Publication Data
A catalogue record for this book is
available from the British Library.

ISBN 0-7445-7256-8

WE LOVE THEM

Written by
Martin Waddell

Illustrated by
Barbara Firth

WALKER BOOKS
AND SUBSIDIARIES
LONDON • BOSTON • SYDNEY

In all the white fields

there was one rabbit.

It was lost.

It was small.

It lay in the snow.

Ben found it.

Ben barked.

We picked it up

and took it home.

Becky thought it would die,

but it didn't.

It lay with Ben.

Ben licked it.

Becky said that Ben thought

it was a little dog, and it thought

Ben was a big rabbit.

They didn't know they'd got it wrong.

Becky said we wouldn't tell them.

We called our rabbit Zoe.

She stayed with Ben.

She played with Ben.

We loved them.

Zoe wasn't little for very long.

She got big…

and bigger…

and bigger still,

but not as big as Ben.

But Ben was old…
and one day
Ben died.

We were sad and
Zoe was sad.
She wouldn't eat her green stuff.
She sat and sat.

There was no Ben for our rabbit,

until one day...

in the pale hay...

there was a puppy.

We took it home.

It lay down with Zoe.

Becky said our puppy thought

Zoe was a dog.

And Zoe thought

our puppy was a rabbit.

They didn't know they'd got it wrong.

Becky said we wouldn't tell them.

The puppy stayed.

The puppy played.

We loved him,

just like we loved Ben.

We called our puppy Little Ben.
But Little Ben got big…
and bigger…
and bigger still.
He got bigger than our rabbit
but not as big as old Ben.

Zoe still thinks

Little Ben is a rabbit,

and Becky says that

Zoe doesn't mind.

Becky says that Zoe

likes big rabbits.

Zoe and Little Ben play
with us in the green fields.
They are our dog
and our rabbit.
We love them.

MORE WALKER PAPERBACKS
For You to Enjoy

Also by Martin Waddell and Barbara Firth

CAN'T YOU SLEEP, LITTLE BEAR?
Winner of the Smarties Book Prize and the Kate Greenaway Medal

"The most perfect children's book ever written or illustrated… It evaporates and dispels all fear of the dark." *Molly Keane, The Sunday Times*

0-7445-1316-2   £4.99

LET'S GO HOME, LITTLE BEAR

Walking through the woods, Little Bear is disturbed by the noises he hears, but Big Bear reassures him.

"An immensely satisfying sequel … gorgeous illustrations." *The Good Book Guide*

0-7445-3169-1   £4.99

YOU AND ME, LITTLE BEAR

While Big Bear works, Little Bear patiently plays his bear games all by himself. What he really wants, though, is for Big Bear to play with him.

"Adorable… A picture book that two to six-year-olds will love." *The Daily Mail*

0-7445-5472-1   £4.99

THE PARK IN THE DARK
Winner of the Kurt Maschler Award

The night-time adventures of three soft-toy animals.

"Absolutely wonderful. The perfect picture book." *Chris Powling, BBC Radio*

0-7445-1740-0   £4.99